The Adventures of LITTLE FUZZY

From the original LITTLE FUZZY by H. Beam Piper

Adapted by Benson Parker

**Illustrated by Michael Whelan
and David Wenzel**

Platt & Munk Publishers/New York
A Division of Grosset & Dunlap

Chapter One

The small, furry creature stomped through the tall grasses to the place where the Big One was working. The bright orange sun burned down across his tiny shoulders, shining on the long, golden hair that covered his body.

As he scrambled along the stream at the bottom of a gorge, he saw again that the water was low. There was less water, less food on Zarathustra every year. The tiny creature forced himself onward to the cliff where the Big One stood. His people, the Gashta, had agreed. If they didn't get the Big Ones to help them, there was no telling what would happen. Still, as the creature crouched beside a bush and lifted his great, green eyes toward the man at the cliff, he shivered with fear. He had never been this close to a Big One before.

He looked to the right and saw the man's aircar parked nearby. He heard him steadily chipping away at the face of the cliff, digging for the shining stones the Big Ones liked so much. The man was a Terran. All the Big Ones on Zarathustra had come from Terra. They came to dig the stones out of the cliffs and sell them to other Big Ones.

The man talked to himself as he worked, speaking in a loud, booming voice. "This'll be a good one," he said. "Worth a thousand sols, at least."

Silently, the Gashta crept down and hid beside the aircar. He watched the man's every move as he worked away beside a red rag that was tied to the face of the cliff. The Big One held up a smooth, yellow stone until it caught the sunlight and began to change colors before his eyes.

For weeks the Gashta had watched him, waiting for his chance. In the morning when the sun was high, the man left the small compound in the woods and came to the cliffs, where he dug for the colored stones until the sun went down again. They were strange creatures, the Big Ones; they worked alone, they lived alone.

The Gashta wondered if the man was lonesome. He understood about that. Gashta got lonely sometimes, too. Lonelier now that there was so little water and food on Zarathustra. There weren't as many of his people now as there once had been.

The Big Ones had to help them. He wasn't sure how, but he would make the man understand. The little creature sighed and shifted his weight anxiously. Even now, many of the Gashta still insisted the Big Ones were bad. They hid themselves from Big Ones and lived secretly in the forest. But maybe—maybe there were some good ones, too.

One thing was for sure: They were a lot different from Gashta. They were as tall as three Gashta squatting on each other's heads, and they had no hair. At least, not very much of it. The Big One working at the cliff had only a little on his face and hardly any at all on his head. They worked a lot, too. It seemed like they were always working at the cliffs, digging out the shining stones, though none of the Gashta could figure out why. But they did seem to have lots of interesting toys. The Gashta were very interested in toys.

It was time. The tiny creature had just decided to stand up and approach the Big One when the whole gorge began to rumble and shake. He screamed as he saw a huge slab of rock slide down the cliff toward the man. Falling debris pelted the trees and splashed in the stream. And even before he had a chance to move, the man and the red rag vanished in a cloud of dust. He threw himself to the ground, covered his head, and waited until the awful shaking of the ground beneath him had quieted. When at last he peered up again through the dust, he saw the Big One on the ground, his leg pinned under a huge, orange rock.

The man didn't move. Silently, the little creature crept toward him. He was sure the man was dead. But then, as he watched him, he saw the man's chest was moving up and down. The Big One was alive!

But he needed help. For a moment, the little Gashta hesitated. What if the Big One woke up and saw him? He slowly scratched his head. He couldn't just leave him there. He would die, or worse, the harpies would come from the woods and get him for sure.

He searched until he found a heavy stick nearby. He grabbed it hurriedly and began to work on the rock. If he could pry it up, he might be able to free the man's ankle. It was hard and dangerous, and the little creature concentrated with all his strength.

At last the huge rock began to budge, and the Gashta reached over and snatched the man's foot from beneath the stone. Then as gently as he could, he grabbed the man by the other ankle and dragged him, little by little, away from the rockslide.

Last of all, he ran back for the man's tool pack and brought it to where he lay, carefully placing the shining yellow stone on top where the Big One was sure to see it when he woke up.

Just then the man stirred and opened his eyes. He blinked slowly in the sunlight, unable to believe what he saw. A small, golden creature with huge, emerald-colored eyes was staring down at him.

"What?" he mumbled. "What the—? Hey! Come back here! I won't hurt you!" He struggled into a sitting position just in time to see the small, fuzzy creature vanish around the bend in the stream.

The Gashta scampered through the woods toward the compound where the Big One lived. There were four small buildings within a fenced-in clearing, and he scurried through a hole in the fence, after making sure there were no other Big Ones around. He crouched down by the side of the main building, and decided to wait there to see if the man made it home. He waited for what seemed like a long time, listening intently for the sound of the aircar. But the Gashta aren't very good at waiting for things, and after a time he peered into the window to see if there was anything interesting inside the Big One's house. The main room was filled with all sorts of strange and wonderful things, and before he knew it, he threw open the window and climbed in.

He ran through the main room into another, smaller one. He stared around him and gasped. One wall held a shiny glass and he saw that he was staring at his own reflection. It was just like looking at himself in a lake. Only instead of bending over, he was standing right in front of it. Next to the glass was a chair with a kind of hole in it, filled with water. He peered into the water in astonishment, but decided not to try to sit on the strange chair. The hole was too big, and he was sure he'd fall right in.

10

There was a curtain in the room, too. And when he pulled it aside and went behind it, he could see bright, shiny handles on the wall. As soon as the little Gashta jumped up to pull on the handles, a magic thing happened. Rain fell all around him. It was much colder than real rain, of course, but it was still rain.

Suddenly a light went on, and before he knew it, he was standing face to face with the Big One.

"Yeek!" he said, and sat down quickly in surprise.

"I thought I saw something like you at the landslide," the Big One said, as he turned off the rain. "Were you the one who helped me out from under that rock?"

The Gashta saw that the man had bandaged his ankle, but he seemed to be all right otherwise. "Yeek," he said, trying to answer the Big One's question.

"I never saw anything like you before. What are you, anyway?"

The man was moving closer and the Gashta watched him uncertainly. It didn't seem like the man wanted to harm him, but it was hard to tell.

"Bet you skipped in when I left the door open, didn't you, Little Fuzzy? That's what you are, sure—a Little Fuzzy."

11

Little Fuzzy rolled his huge eyes. Not exactly, Big One, he thought.

But the man was still talking. "Well, if a Little Fuzzy finds a door open, I'd like to know why he shouldn't come in and look around."

Well, he got that part right, thought Little Fuzzy.

The man reached out to touch Little Fuzzy, who jumped in surprise. Then he reached out slowly and touched the man's shirt. It felt funny. Poor Big One, he thought, he doesn't have hair all over him and so he has to make things to cover himself. And he didn't do a very good job. It doesn't feel like hair at all. By the way the man was petting his arm, Little Fuzzy could tell the Big One thought his fur felt better than his old shirt.

"Why sure, we're going to be friends, aren't we? Would you like something to eat? Suppose you and I go see what we can find."

And before Little Fuzzy could do anything about it, the Big One picked him up and started carrying him to another part of the house. Little Fuzzy was insulted and angry. Just because the Big One was bigger than he was, didn't mean he could go carrying him around. He kicked and hit and struggled, but the man kept talking to him, and after awhile, Little Fuzzy decided being carried wasn't so bad after all. It felt kind of nice, actually.

"Now, what does a Little Fuzzy like to eat?" the Big One asked. "Open your mouth and let Pappy Jack see what you have to chew with."

Little Fuzzy opened his mouth and then shut it quick.

"You're probably omnivorous." Pappy Jack rubbed his chin. "That means you'll eat just about anything. How would you like some nice Terran Federation Space Forces Emergency Ration?"

"Yeek!" said Little Fuzzy. He was very hungry. But he could tell that Pappy Jack didn't understand a thing he said. Not only was Pappy Jack furless, but his ears probably weren't made right, either.

Pappy Jack put him carefully down on the kitchen floor, and Little Fuzzy watched as he opened a tin of something and broke off a piece of whatever was inside. Pappy Jack handed him some golden-brown cake and Little Fuzzy smelled it carefully. It smelled delicious, like tree bark in the woods. "Yeek," he said appreciatively. But Pappy Jack still didn't understand him. So Little Fuzzy crammed the whole piece into his mouth at once.

Pappy Jack smiled, "You never had to live on that stuff for a whole month and nothing else, that's for sure." Then he gave Little Fuzzy a big portion of the cake on a plate and a cup full of water.

Fuzzy chewed happily and watched Pappy Jack, who then lit a small fire and put it against a strange thing sticking out of his mouth. He couldn't believe his eyes when he saw Pappy Jack suck on his pipe and blow out smoke! Big Ones really were strange.

When he was finished eating, he ran to explore the big room. There were all sorts of wonderful things there. He found a big basket and dumped it out on the floor. He played happily with the things in the basket until Pappy Jack came out of the kitchen and caught him.

"No, Little Fuzzy," Pappy Jack said. "You do not dump out wastebaskets and then walk away from them. You put things back." Pappy Jack touched the basket and said, very distinctly, "Waste . . . basket."

This is silly, thought Little Fuzzy. I can understand him fine. It's he who can't understand me.

But he watched as Pappy Jack righted the wastebasket and picked up a piece of paper and threw it in. Then he handed Little Fuzzy a piece of paper and said, "Waste . . . basket."

"What's the matter with you, Pappy Jack?" Little Fuzzy asked. But he could tell that Pappy Jack hadn't understood him at all. So Little Fuzzy picked up everything on the floor and threw it back into the wastebasket, all except a bright red plastic box and a bottle with a cap.

"Yeek?" He held the things up so Pappy Jack would get the point.

"Yes, you can have them. You know, you're a smart little thing. I'm going to tell Ben Rainsford about you."

Little Fuzzy watched as Pappy Jack went to a big screen and punched some keys. And all at once, a wonderful thing happened. There was a man in the room talking to Pappy Jack. Well, he wasn't exactly in the room—Little Fuzzy could see he was on the screen. But just to make sure, he went carefully up to the man and touched him. He looked at Pappy Jack. "Yeek?" he said, pointing to the new Big One.

"That's Ben, Little Fuzzy. Now come on over by me." Little Fuzzy went and climbed up on to Pappy Jack's lap.

The man on the screen started to speak. "Hi, Jack." he said. "What's new in your neck of the woods?"

Pappy Jack smiled. "Well, Ben, since you're the expert on Zarathustran life, I thought I'd give you a call and see what you thought of my little friend here."

Ben studied the small furry creature that lay in Pappy Jack's arms. "What have you got there? Some new kind of water dog?"

Little Fuzzy sat straight up. Some kind of water dog indeed! Pappy Jack said, "No Ben, I don't think so. This little guy might just be a new species. He seems as though he's intelligent anyway."

The man on the screen looked shocked. "You mean a sapient?"

"I honestly don't know, Ben. Why don't you come out to the compound and have a look?"

Ben consulted a small calendar on his desk. "I have to make a run to the outpost at the north end of the Great Woods, but I think I can make it to your place within the next couple of days."

Pappy Jack smiled. "Great, Ben. See you then."

When Pappy Jack finished talking to the man, he made the pictures on the screen change. "Now," he said, "we'll see something nice."

But instead what Little Fuzzy saw was a raging forest fire. It scared him so much that he threw his arms around Pappy Jack's neck and buried his face in his shirt. Pappy Jack quickly changed the picture and looked at Little Fuzzy in surprise. Well, forest fires started from lightning sometimes and they were bad things for a Gashta. What did Pappy Jack expect, anyway?

When he looked up again at the screen there was a beautiful sunset and music playing. Little Fuzzy relaxed against Pappy Jack and snuggled closer. All in all, he thought it was a good thing he'd decided to rescue the Big One today. Pappy Jack's was a fun place, and Pappy Jack wasn't so bad—even if he was a Big One. Little Fuzzy sighed happily and watched the things on the screen with his new friend until he fell asleep.

Chapter Two

The next morning at daylight, Little Fuzzy was busily trying to dig Pappy Jack out from under the covers. Pappy Jack looked at him sleepily. "Little Fuzzy," he said, "you are, unfortunately, a first-rate alarm clock." But Little Fuzzy only looked at him and said, "Yeek?" He couldn't understand about Big Ones. Everything on Zarathustra got up with the sun.

He played at Pappy Jack's most of the morning and didn't get bored once. He screwed and unscrewed nuts and bolts and bottle tops, and found any number of toys around the Big One's house. When Pappy Jack went out of the room for a minute, he even tried to smoke Pappy Jack's pipe. But it tasted awful.

Later, after they had had some more of the tree-bark food, Pappy Jack showed him a collection of sunstones. At least, that's what Pappy Jack said they were. Little Fuzzy laid the stones out in circles and spirals—all the time trying to show Pappy Jack where there were other Fuzzies living on Zarathustra. He took some stones away in parts of the pattern to show him where a great many Fuzzies had died. But though he played the game over and over, Pappy Jack still didn't understand. He would have to find another way to tell him about the Gashta. Finally, he put the stones back into the tin and rolled it onto the bed Pappy Jack had made for him the night before. He put the tin next to the red plastic box and the bottle with the cap.

But even though he couldn't make Pappy Jack understand about the Gashta, Little Fuzzy decided that Pappy Jack was one of the good Big ones. He liked to play and gave him delicious food and a warm place to sleep. Besides, he had lots and lots of toys.

That night, as Little Fuzzy lay on his bed and listened to the snoring from the other room, he thought of another way to tell Pappy Jack about the Gashta. And so the next day, when Pappy Jack had returned to the gorge to mine sunstones, Little Fuzzy set off for the woods. Later, Pappy Jack had quite a surprise when he saw his Little Fuzzy returning to the compound with five more Fuzzies and a baby Fuzzy in tow.

"So! That's why you ran off and worried Pappy Jack? You wanted your family here, too!" Pappy Jack was smiling at the sight of them.

Very slowly one of the Fuzzies came over and touched Pappy Jack's shirt, then reached up and pulled his moustache. Before long, all of them were climbing on Pappy Jack, even the baby, who was small enough to fit on his palm. But in less than a minute, Baby had climbed to his shoulder and was sitting right on Pappy Jack's head!

After they were all acquainted, Pappy Jack said, "Well, this calls for a party. You people want dinner?"

Little Fuzzy yeeked emphatically and Pappy Jack led them all into the kitchen. They ate cold roast veldbeest, yummiyams and lots and lots of fried pool-ball fruit.

After dinner they all went back into the living room. Baby Fuzzy climbed up and right away sat on Pappy Jack's head. The rest of the family chased and punched each other, yeeking happily. Pappy Jack looked happy, too. When he'd returned from the mine and found Little Fuzzy gone, he thought he'd lost him for good. But now he had six Fuzzies and a Baby to keep him company.

Pappy Jack lit his pipe and started to name the Fuzzies. There was Little Fuzzy, Mama and Baby. Those names came easy. Pappy Jack then named the three who looked like each other, Max, Mike and Mitzi, and the one who liked to run and jump so much he named Ko-Ko. Little Fuzzy decided that names must be important to the Big Ones. He thought it would be nice to someday find out what all the strange names meant. Maybe by then they would have found a way to get the Big Ones to understand them.

Late the next afternoon two more Big Ones came to the compound in an aircar. Little Fuzzy had seen them before from the woods, and thought they must be Pappy Jack's friends.

"It's Star Sheriff George," Pappy Jack said, as a big man climbed down from the aircar, "and the prize-winning police force of the planet Zarathustra!"

From his place at the window, Little Fuzzy studied the Big Ones' faces and decided that that must be a joke. Everyone was smiling, so he smiled, too.

"No trouble?" asked George. "We're just on the rounds, and thought we'd drop in to see how you're making out. Haven't had any problems lately, have you?"

"Not a one," answered Pappy Jack. "But hang up your guns for a minute. There's something I want to show you."

Just then Little Fuzzy scampered across the yard to meet the new Big Ones in the blue clothes.

He pulled at Pappy Jack's trouser leg.

"I think your *something* wants some attention," one of the new Big Ones said. Little Fuzzy studied him closely. He had kind eyes and more hair on his face than Pappy Jack. "How about it, little one, will you come to me?"

The man extended his arms and picked him up. At that point the rest of the Fuzzies decided it was safe to come and meet the Big Ones, and they all ran out into the yard.

George took a few steps backward at the sight of them. "Hey, Jack, what are these things, anyway?"

Pappy Jack looked surprised. "Fuzzies. Mean to tell me you've never seen Fuzzies before?"

"No, I haven't. What are they?"

"I just told you. Fuzzies. That's the only name I know for them. You're the constable, I thought you'd know."

A couple of the Fuzzies came over and looked interestedly at George. One of them pointed to him and said, "Yeek?"

Pappy Jack smiled and translated. "They want to know what you are."

Little Fuzzy jumped down then, and George's friend picked up Mama Fuzzy. "Never saw anything like them before, Jack." he said. "Where did they come from?"

"Ahmed, you don't know anything about them and you shouldn't be picking them up. They could give you a disease," said George.

"They won't hurt me, Lieutenant. They haven't hurt Jack, have they?" Then Ahmed sat right down on the ground with all the Fuzzies. George stared at Ahmed for a minute, and then, because he wouldn't let any of his men do anything he was afraid to do himself, he sat down, too. Little Fuzzy thought this was funny and laughed until Mama frowned at him and cuffed him for being rude. Mama brought the baby to George, and Baby immediately crawled up and sat on his head.

"Well—they are cute little fellows," George admitted. Then Little Fuzzy grabbed George's police whistle and began to blow on it. Little Fuzzy ran into the house with Mike and Mitzi close at his heels, trying to get the whistle away from him. It was a wonderful game, sliding across the floor and diving around corners.

"We have a whole shoebox full of whistles at the post," George shouted above the din. "We'll just give them these two, all right?"

When things had calmed down a bit, George asked, "What are you going to do with them, Jack?"

"I've told Ben Rainsford about them, and he's going to come out and have a look at them in a couple of days."

"He's the expert on Zarathustran life forms?" asked Ahmed.

"That's the one," said Pappy Jack. "This is going to knock his socks off."

Two days later, when Pappy Jack returned from a day of mining, he found Ben Rainsford sitting on the bench by the kitchen door. Little Fuzzy came over and tugged on Pappy Jack's trouser leg. "Yeek," he said, pointing to Ben. Ben was surrounded by Fuzzies. Baby Fuzzy was sitting on his head, and there were two new Fuzzies.

Little Fuzzzy pointed again to the new Fuzzies, who had stopped playing when Pappy Jack came, and were standing shyly behind the bench.

"We have two new Fuzzies?"

"Yeek," said Little Fuzzy and dragged him closer. Little Fuzzy then folded his arms authoritatively across his chest and said, "Yeek."

"All right, they can stay, too. But let's give them names."

Little Fuzzy rolled his eyes. Names again.

"Let me see—we'll call them Goldilocks and Cinderella because they're so pretty."

Little Fuzzy was happy with that.

"Well, Ben, what do you think of them?" Pappy Jack asked.

"Don't start me on that, Jack. I stopped by the constabulary post; when George told me more about them, I thought he was the biggest liar in the galaxy."

"This is Little Fuzzy. He brought the rest: Mama, Baby, Max, Mike, Mitzi, and Ko-Ko. These two are new."

"Would you mind," asked Ben, "if I brought some people from the capital to see them? I think they'd be very interested."

Pappy Jack looked a little uncertain. But he said, "I think the Fuzzies would like that all right. They like company."

When they all went inside, Little Fuzzy jumped up on the armchair and switched on the viewscreen. He fiddled with the selector until he got the big Blackwater woods-burning that Pappy Jack had showed him before. Mike and Mitzy shrieked delightedly and Little Fuzzy listened as they explained to Goldilocks and Cinderella that there was nothing to be afraid of. It wasn't really happening. They knew by now that nothing from the screen could get out and hurt them.

Little Fuzzy wandered into the kitchen where Ben and Pappy Jack were sitting at the table. He climbed up and sat between them. They were having a serious conversation and he wanted to know what it was all about.

"They can come," Pappy Jack was telling Ben, "as long as these little people are treated with respect. You will not let anyone hurt them or annoy them or make them do anything they don't want to do?" He rubbed Little Fuzzy's neck affectionately. "Nothing will happen to you, Little Fuzzy," he said. "Pappy Jack will take care of you." But Little Fuzzy thought Pappy Jack was trying hard to reassure himself, and he shivered a little.

"I understand that." said Ben. "Is there anything you'd like them to bring out?"

"Yes, a few things for the camp. Three cases of Extee Three."

"That stuff? Why Emergency Rations?"

Pappy Jack shrugged. "I don't know, they love it."

Ben studied Little Fuzzy for a moment. "They do seem awfully hungry. Maybe that's why they've decided to come out of the woods. Maybe food is scarce."

Pappy Jack nodded in agreement. "And if the drought continues, it's going to get even harder to find," he said. "Oh, yeah, and tell them to bring some toys. Just think of what you'd like if you were a Little Fuzzy and bring it along."

Chapter Three

Soon there were lots of people at the compound where before there had just been Pappy Jack. There was Gerd and Ruth from the Science Center, and Ben. And then there was Mr. Kellogg. Nobody seemed to like Mr. Kellogg, even though Pappy Jack sold him his sunstones whenever he came to the compound.

Tuesday was hot and windless, even at dawn. Little Fuzzy stood by himself and watched the red sun rise in a hard, brassy sky.

"I don't like it, either," said Mama Fuzzy in answer to his thoughts as she came out of the main house with Ko-Ko and Cinderella.

Cinderella agreed. "Things happen when the sun rises like that, all red and bloody."

"Superstitious, that's all." Ko-Ko executed some experimental swipes with the new chopper-digger that Pappy Jack had made him. Suddenly he stopped. "But there is that Mr. Kellogg. I don't trust him."

"Nor do I," said Little Fuzzy as he paced the ground slowly. "But Pappy Jack is responsible to him, in a way. He sells his shining stones to Kellogg."

"But he is one of the bad Big Ones—I can feel it." Ko-Ko stabbed at the air with his weapon, forcing Little Fuzzy to dodge one of his more exuberant swings.

Pappy Jack walked by his window and looked at the Fuzzies out in the yard. They were so lovable, just like children. At any rate, they seemed to be discussing something, and Pappy Jack wondered briefly if those little yeeks of theirs weren't some kind of language.

"But I'm sure Mr. Kellogg doesn't mean to be bad," Mama was saying. "He just doesn't understand about the Gashta."

"I don't know about that," Little Fuzzy retorted. "He wants the Big Ones to believe we are animals—like water dogs or land prawns."

"It's true!" cried Max. I heard him talking to one of the Big Ones from the capital on the screen!"

"That can't be true." cried Mama. "Besides, we have convinced them we are like them—like Big Ones."

"That's not the point. Everyone in the compound knows that we are a sapient race of beings. But if Mr. Kellogg should convince the Big Ones in the cities and even on Terra that we are not, we would not have our own ways anymore. We would be slaves to the Big Ones. They would become the rulers of Zarathustra. And Mr. Kellogg would have lots of cheap labor for his mines. He could make us dig for stones."

"What mines?"

"The shining stone mines—the sunstone mines."

Cinderella, Ko-Ko and Mama stood very still and thought hard. "Perhaps," Cinderella said uncertainly.

"There is no perhaps." Little Fuzzy shrugged impatiently. "And there's more. Haven't you noticed they're always touching us?"

"Well—you're right about that."

"Well—think about it."

"I don't get it."

Little Fuzzy narrowed his huge eyes for a moment. "Mr. Kellogg could make a lot of money on Terra by importing Fuzzy fur," he announced gravely. The others stared at him, horrified.

"Pappy Jack and the others won't let that happen," Mama said firmly. "They like Gashta."

"The one called Kellogg doesn't," said Little Fuzzy. What he didn't say was that Mr. Kellogg made him feel afraid.

After breakfast Ruth and Gerd went for a walk, and as they came across the footbridge toward the compound, Little Fuzzy, Ko-Ko and Goldilocks ran to meet them. Ruth picked up Goldilocks and carried her while the others ran ahead.

"This one is my favorite," Ruth told Gerd. "She is the sweetest of them all. Of course," she said as she bent down and chucked Little Fuzzy under the chin, "they're all pretty nice."

Goldilocks began to play with the silver charm on Ruth's necklace. She shook it and it made small tinkling sounds. She held it up to Ruth and asked, "Yeek?"

"Yes, sweetie, you can have it." Ruth took off her necklace with one hand and held Goldilocks with the other. She had to loop the necklace around three times before it would fit her small, fuzzy neck. "There now, that's your very own."

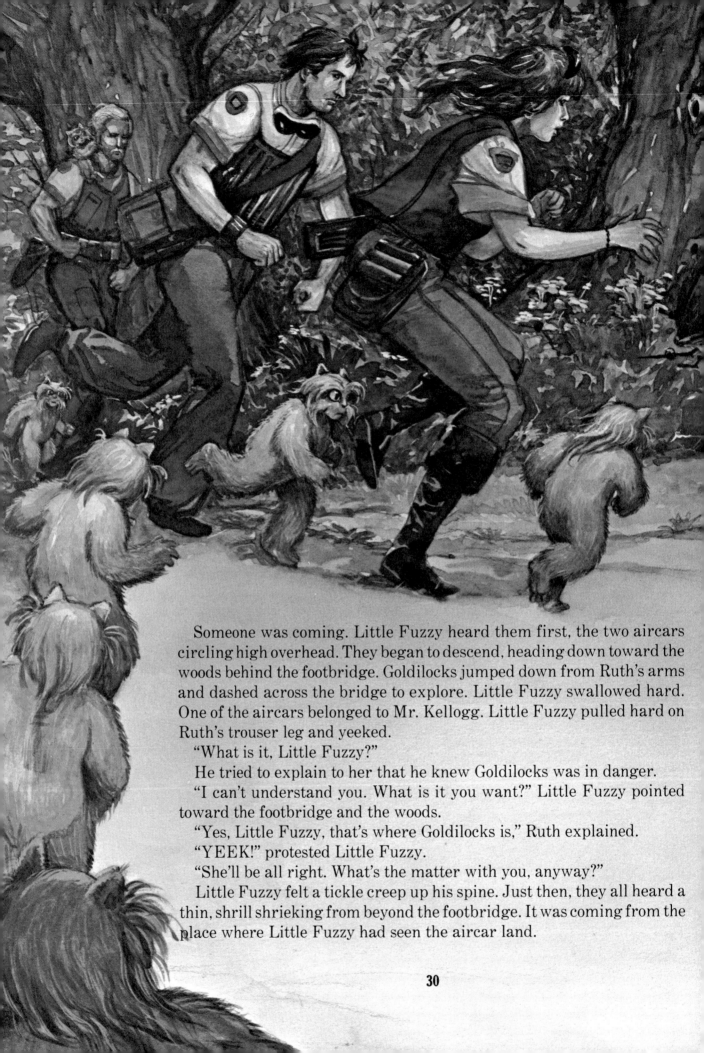

Someone was coming. Little Fuzzy heard them first, the two aircars circling high overhead. They began to descend, heading down toward the woods behind the footbridge. Goldilocks jumped down from Ruth's arms and dashed across the bridge to explore. Little Fuzzy swallowed hard. One of the aircars belonged to Mr. Kellogg. Little Fuzzy pulled hard on Ruth's trouser leg and yeeked.

"What is it, Little Fuzzy?"

He tried to explain to her that he knew Goldilocks was in danger.

"I can't understand you. What is it you want?" Little Fuzzy pointed toward the footbridge and the woods.

"Yes, Little Fuzzy, that's where Goldilocks is," Ruth explained.

"YEEK!" protested Little Fuzzy.

"She'll be all right. What's the matter with you, anyway?"

Little Fuzzy felt a tickle creep up his spine. Just then, they all heard a thin, shrill shrieking from beyond the footbridge. It was coming from the place where Little Fuzzy had seen the aircar land.

They all raced across the footbridge in a group, Big Ones, Fuzzies and even Pappy Jack, who had rushed outside to see what the commotion was about.

But when they reached the clearing, all they found was the one called Kellogg, standing near an aircar with a stupid grin on his face, his hand still on the butt of his disintegrator gun. There were Fuzzy tracks all around him, but no Goldilocks.

"Where's Goldilocks?" demanded Ruth.

Mr. Kellogg scratched his head. "Now, let me see, which one is that?"

"You know very well which one. Where is she?" Ruth stared Kellogg in the eye, her hands clenched into fists at her sides.

"I don't know. That little beast attacked me!"

"That's ridiculous. She probably just wanted you to see her new jingle, that's all."

"It attacked me and ran off, that's all I know," Kellogg insisted. He pulled up his trouser leg to show them. "It gave me a serious wound. You can see for yourself."

Everyone looked except Ruth, who was searching the edge of the clearing for some sign of Goldilocks. To Little Fuzzy, Mr. Kellogg's wound looked like nothing but a briar scratch.

"You bully," Ruth had found something in the bushes and was stalking over to Kellogg, twirling something in her hand. "Look at this," she held the necklace aloft for the others to see. "I gave this to Goldilocks a little while ago. And I happen to know she wouldn't have taken it off unless she was forced to—or worse." Ruth threw the necklace to the ground at Kellogg's feet. And all at once, she began to cry.

Little Fuzzy gulped hard. Ruth was right. He was sure something bad had happened to Goldilocks and she was gone for good. He turned away and toward the southeast horizon saw the blue constabulary car about to land. He heard Pappy Jack muttering to himself. "Never here when you need them."

The one called George climbed out of his aircar and his smile faded immediately when he saw the grim faces all around him. "What's going on?" he asked "Anybody need anything?"

Ruth, Pappy Jack and Mr. Kellogg pulled George over to one side and began whispering angrily. Mr. Kellogg grew red in the face and began to shout at them. "Let the court decide, then! They'll back me up against the little beasts!"

George looked steadily at Mr. Kellogg. "We will, Kellogg," he said. "But I'd be careful if I were you. You might find yourself charged with murder."

Mr. Kellogg gave George an ugly look. "Nobody is going to believe that these things are any better than dogs!"

Everyone started sadly back to the compound. Pappy Jack scooped Little Fuzzy up on one shoulder. "Looks like you're going to court, my friend."

"Yeek?"

"We have to prove that Fuzzies have the same rights as humans on Zarathustra. And fast. Once we do that, you'll be protected against *accidents.*"

Little Fuzzy had no idea what court was. But from the look in Pappy Jack's eyes, one thing was for sure. Mr. Kellogg would not be able to bother them any more.

Chapter Four

Late that evening, they heard a constabulary siren echoing over the camp. Little Fuzzy looked up interestedly. He knew that sound. That was George and the other Big Ones in the blue clothes.

Pappy Jack went to the door. "Hello, George," he said. "Come on in."

George looked unhappy. "We have to talk to you, Jack. At least these men do." George frowned and looked at the floor.

Something was wrong—Little Fuzzy could tell. And for the second time that day, he felt a tickle of fear creep along his spine.

"Jack," George said, holding a piece of paper in front of Pappy Jack, "this is a court order to impound your Fuzzies as evidence in the Kellogg vs. Fuzzies case. These men are from the Central courts; they've been ordered to take the Fuzzies into the capital."

"Let me see that," Pappy Jack's forehead crinkled as he frowned at the paper. "They have to take the Fuzzies," he announced to the others. "There's nothing I can do."

As if by some secret signal, all the Fuzzies began to run at once. The men from the constabulary chased them around the house and grounds until at last they were all squirming in rough canvas sacks, whimpering softly. Little Fuzzy felt himself being carried out of Pappy Jack's house and into the aircar and there was nothing he could do about it.

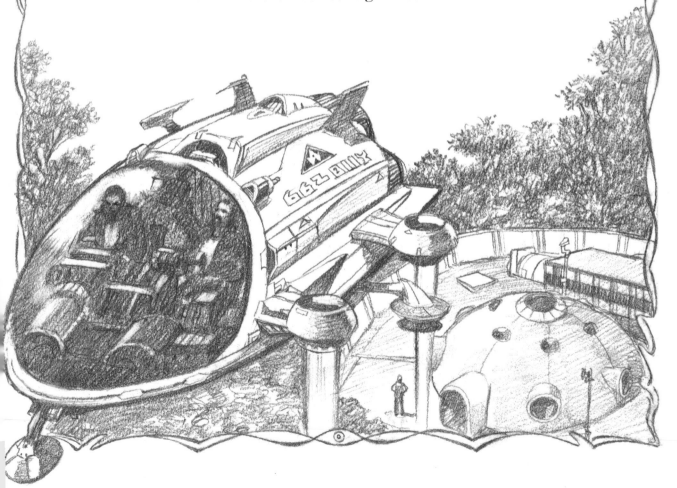

Little Fuzzy didn't understand. The ones in blue clothes had been good to the Fuzzies—given them whistles. And why had Pappy Jack not stopped them? He thought and thought as they rose up in the aircar and shot into the sky at a dizzying speed. It couldn't be that Pappy Jack was afraid. He wasn't afraid of anything.

He listened closely and knew that the others were near.

"Yeek?" he asked. In the soft darkness he could hear six answering yeeks.

"Why did Pappy Jack betray us?" asked Cinderella.

"What do we do now?" asked Mama.

"I'm here, too. Are you, Mitzi?" said Mike.

"Yes, how do we get out of these bags?"

Little Fuzzy found the edge of the knife Pappy Jack had made for him when he first came to the camp. He could cut his way out of the bag now and free the others, but while they were still in the aircar, it would be no use; they would be caught immediately. Better to wait.

"Wait," he told the others.

"But where are they taking us?"

"How will we find Pappy Jack again?"

"Wait." he said again. And they all sped into the darkness. Away from the compound, and Pappy Jack, and the great, green woods of Zarathustra.

Little Fuzzy was the last one to be let out of his canvas sack. He could hear the others around him, yeeking sadly. He yeeked back, trying to tell them not to be too upset. Just then a Big One picked him up and roughly plopped him into a wire cage. There were splinters on the floor and they hurt his feet.

"Yeek?" he asked the Big One.

But the man only stared at him for a moment before locking his cage and leaving him alone. Little Fuzzy looked around him; all the rest were there, crouched on the floors of their separate cages staring at him with huge, emerald-colored eyes. And over them all a tiny light cast a sad, blue-white glow.

Little Fuzzy sat absolutely still until he was sure everyone had gone. He listened to the others, their soft whimpering echoing in the empty room. They were waiting, just as he had told them to do—waiting to see what he would do next.

When he was sure they had been left alone for the night, he got out the little spring steel knife that Pappy Jack had made for him and held it up. Blue-white light caught the blade and the other Fuzzies gasped. Carefully Little Fuzzy began to cut away at his prison. The soft wire cut easily, and it wasn't long before Little Fuzzy had cut away the wire netting at the frame in a corner of his cage. Silently he bent it back in a triangle just big enough for a Fuzzy to crawl through.

He slipped out of his cage and onto the floor and everyone whispered excitedly. Then he crept toward Ko-Ko's cage. The Big Ones had slipped a bolt through the door and screwed it closed with nuts. Hurriedly Little Fuzzy unscrewed the nut and slipped out the bolt. It was as easy as playing with bottle tops at Pappy Jack's. Ko-Ko grinned happily and opened the door with a flying kick. The two of them hurried to the other cages to free Max, Mike, Mitzi, Cinderella and Mama.

When they were all out, they dragged Ko-Ko's cage over to a door that led to another room. Little Fuzzy stood on top of the cage to reach the spring lock that opened it. That was easy, too. It was just like the spring locks at Pappy Jack's.

One by one, the Fuzzies scampered over the top of the cage and jumped down into the next room. Even in the dim light, Little Fuzzy knew it was an office. It looked almost like Pappy Jack's office at the compound, with a big desk and lots of papers piled up. Little Fuzzy looked around for a really bad thing he could do to the room. Then he saw the wastebasket. As fast as he could, he dumped the wastebasket and left it dumped. Ko-Ko climbed on top of the desk and threw everything off it—papers, books, pencils—until it was completely bare. Max and Cinderella emptied out all of the drawers and files, and Mike and Mitzi helped by scattering everything around as much as they could. Little Fuzzy looked around the room and grinned. That would teach the Big Ones to try and lock up a Fuzzy. Then Mama pushed the desk chair over to the door and Little Fuzzy climbed up and unlocked the latch.

In no time at all they were running down a narrow hall. For the first time Little Fuzzy really began to be afraid. He hadn't any idea where to go.

They ran through a huge, scary room full of glass cases. Every case had an animal in it, and even though they were standing, it looked to Little Fuzzy like they were dead. He wanted a closer look but just then Mama ran smack into a case that held a huge, Zarathustran harpy. Harpies liked to eat Fuzzies and she screamed until Little Fuzzy took her hand and pulled her away.

Was that why the Big Ones had brought them here? Did they want to kill them and put them in glass cases and bring them to court dead?

Little Fuzzy gulped. He couldn't let that happen. Maybe Big Ones were not so good after all, even if they did have good toys. You never knew what they were going to do. You could never tell what they were thinking. You couldn't trust them. Little Fuzzy was thinking hard about that when he ran smack into Ruth's legs. He looked up at her and yeeked. They were really in trouble now. He could tell by the look on her face that she had been coming to get them.

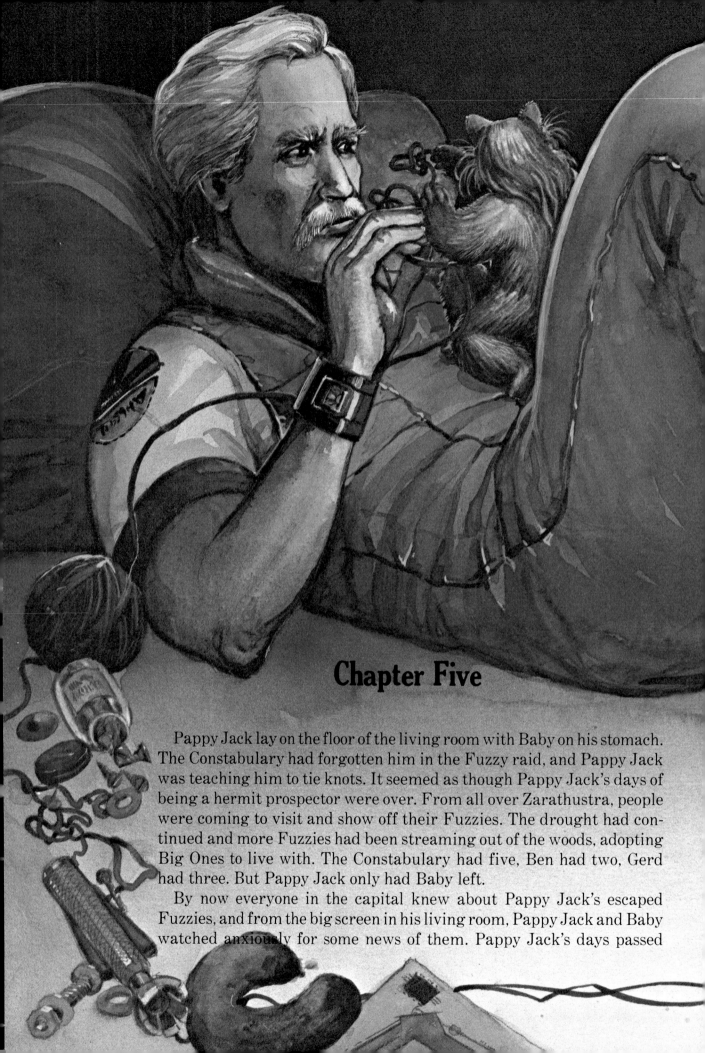

Chapter Five

Pappy Jack lay on the floor of the living room with Baby on his stomach. The Constabulary had forgotten him in the Fuzzy raid, and Pappy Jack was teaching him to tie knots. It seemed as though Pappy Jack's days of being a hermit prospector were over. From all over Zarathustra, people were coming to visit and show off their Fuzzies. The drought had continued and more Fuzzies had been streaming out of the woods, adopting Big Ones to live with. The Constabulary had five, Ben had two, Gerd had three. But Pappy Jack only had Baby left.

By now everyone in the capital knew about Pappy Jack's escaped Fuzzies, and from the big screen in his living room, Pappy Jack and Baby watched anxiously for some news of them. Pappy Jack's days passed

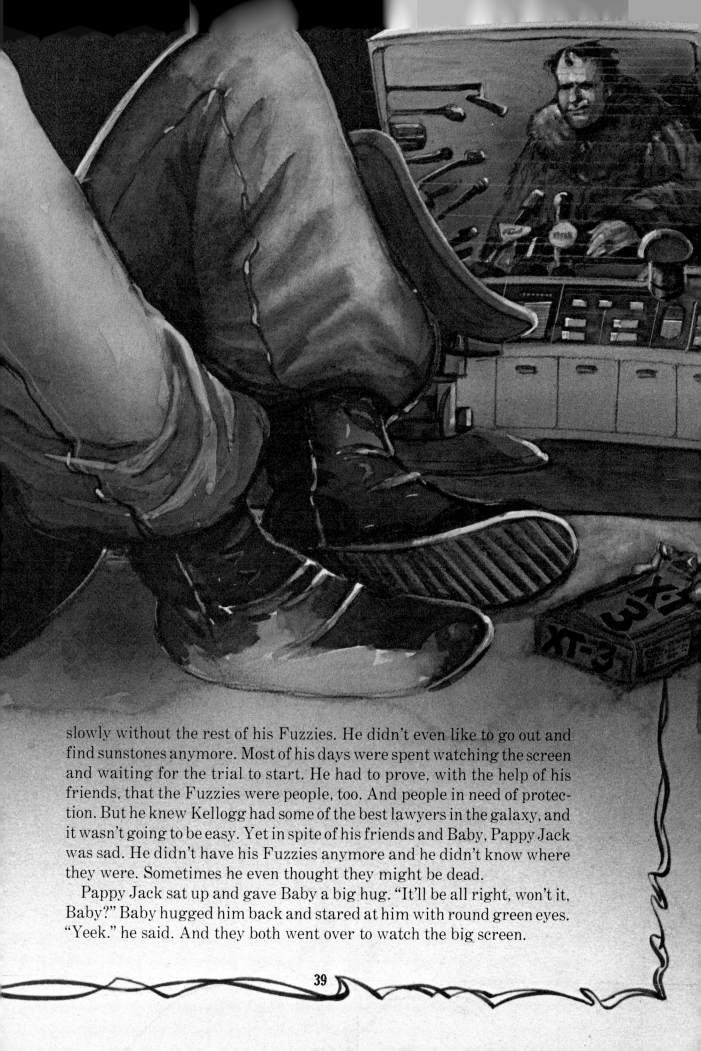

slowly without the rest of his Fuzzies. He didn't even like to go out and find sunstones anymore. Most of his days were spent watching the screen and waiting for the trial to start. He had to prove, with the help of his friends, that the Fuzzies were people, too. And people in need of protection. But he knew Kellogg had some of the best lawyers in the galaxy, and it wasn't going to be easy. Yet in spite of his friends and Baby, Pappy Jack was sad. He didn't have his Fuzzies anymore and he didn't know where they were. Sometimes he even thought they might be dead.

Pappy Jack sat up and gave Baby a big hug. "It'll be all right, won't it, Baby?" Baby hugged him back and stared at him with round green eyes. "Yeek." he said. And they both went over to watch the big screen.

On the first day of the trial, Pappy Jack, Baby and Gerd got into the aircar and went to the capital to appear in court. Baby yeeked excitedly as they flew over the sprawling city. The first day of the trial wasn't much fun for Pappy Jack, but Baby had a wonderful time.

Right away Baby found himself in the viewfinder and waved. He drew pictures all over Pappy Jack's notes and sat on his head and made faces at the judge.

They announced in court that there was a reward out for Pappy Jack's Fuzzies. No one seemed to know where they were. Then a few people took the stand and declared that they had seen the escaped Fuzzies.

Baby wanted to ask Pappy Jack why they had to stay here and listen to all these strange people talk all day. Baby thought that being in the compound was much nicer than being here. But Pappy Jack couldn't understand what Baby said, and told him to shush and stop all those yeeks. He wanted to hear what the judge was saying.

The second day of the trial was much better. The Space Navy was called in to testify and they brought with them some battery-powered hearing aids. As one of the officers passed out the devices to the court, another one spoke up:

"Your honor, we have made a momentous discovery in connection with the Fuzzies."

Carefully, Pappy Jack adjusted his hearing aid, while Baby tried his best to get his new toy away from him. He was still yelling at Pappy Jack when Pappy Jack put the plug into his ear and switched on the power for the first time. He stared at Baby incredulously as he heard a number of small sounds he had never heard before. Baby was talking to him!

"*Heinta sawaaka igg sa geeda.*"

Pappy Jack jumped up and cried, "He's talking! Ultrasonic. Their language is ultrasonic! Why didn't we think of that a long time ago?"

Pappy Jack shut off his hearing aid. Baby Fuzzy was saying, "Yeek?"

When he turned it on again, Baby was saying, "*Kukkina za zeeva.*"

Pappy Jack gave Baby a big hug.

"Oh, Baby, Pappy Jack doesn't understand. We'll have to be patient and learn each other's language."

"*Pappee Jaack?*" Baby cried. "*Babee Zehinga. Pappee Jaack za zag ga heizza.*"

"Mr. Holloway," the judge was saying. "May we have your attention?"

Pappy Jack turned to the judge with a big smile. This proved it.

Animals didn't have language, only people had language. The Fuzzies *were* people. Just like he'd said all along.

And that's when the best thing of all happened. A constable left the room and when he came back, he brought seven Fuzzies into the court. They stood in a huddle in the middle of the room and stared around them. From his place at the table, Pappy Jack stared back. It couldn't be, but there they were. Little Fuzzy, Mama, Max, Mike, Mitzi, Ko-Ko and Cinderella. Baby whooped and ran to Mama. Then they saw him and ran to him, yelling, *"Pappe Jaack! Pappee Jaack!"*

The judge banged his gavel and called for a recess, while Pappy Jack sat on the floor with his Fuzzies, hugging every one.

Little Fuzzy tried to explain that they had been safe with Ruth and the Space Navy, but finally had to give up because of all the noise. Then they showed Pappy Jack what the Navy had given them. Each of the Fuzzies wore a little shoulder bag printed with the name, "Marines." They opened the bags to show Pappy Jack what was inside. There were bolts and screws and red plastic bottles with tops, and toothbrushes, pens, pencils and a small flashlight for each of them.

Pappy Jack turned to the Space Navy captain. "Captain Grebenfeld, I want to thank you for taking care of my Fuzzies. And I'm very glad you discovered their ultrasonic speech. But why couldn't you have let me know they were safe? I haven't been very happy this past month, you know."

The Captain's face softened. "I know it, Mr. Holloway, and we were all sorry for you, but we couldn't risk compromising our agent in the Intelligence Center who smuggled the Fuzzies out."

Ruth walked up behind the captain with a twinkle in her eye. "That's right, Jack. They couldn't." Ruth looked at Jack and put a finger to her lips. "Right?"

Pappy Jack smiled. "It was you?" he asked. Ruth grinned in agreement.

That night Pappy Jack threw a big party for all his friends and all the Fuzzies. It was a happy celebration, and everyone stayed up far too late and ate entirely too much ice cream, cake, cookies and Extee Three.

Chapter Six

But the case wasn't over yet. The next day, everyone was allowed to sit together in court. It took the Fuzzies a few minutes to learn that when the judge banged his gavel, they all had to sit very still and not talk. But Baby never learned. He was always scurrying around with Mama running after him.

When Ruth took the stand, the Fuzzies burst into applause.

"On the night of the twenty-second," she began, "when the Fuzzies were taken from Mr. Holloway, they were immediately brought to the Science Center and put in cages. They escaped at once. I found them in the hall and brought them to Commander Aelborg who had taken charge of the operation and was sworn to study them in secrecy in the Space Naval Center. It was our intention to test the Fuzzies for intelligence—to prove scientifically that the Fuzzies are sapient beings and entitled to the same rights as people."

"And to what conclusion have you come?" asked the judge.

"The discovery that their language is ultrasonic, that in fact they have a language at all proves conclusively that the Fuzzies are people, Your Honor. Language is used as a criteria of sapience throughout the galaxy."

Pappy Jack stood up. "This is a criminal court, Your Honor. What about Kellogg?"

Everyone turned to look at Mr. Kellogg, who was sitting across the room. Slowly he rose and addressed the court. "I—" he began, and faltered.

Mama ran to him and patted him on the hand. "All Goldilocks wanted to do," she tried to tell him, "was to show you her new jingle."

43

Mr. Kellogg looked at Mama for a moment, then buried his face in his hands. Two constabulary corporals came and led him slowly out of the courtroom.

The next day in court there was so much discussion between the judge and the lawyers that no one paid any attention at all to the Fuzzies. And so before long they got a little bit bored and decided to have some fun. After all, a Fuzzy couldn't be expected to sit still all the time, could he?

One of the constabulary's Fuzzies crept out into the hall and came back in, dragging a piece of air hose that he'd found. He sauntered into the open space between the tables and beckoned for the other Fuzzies to come and join him. Ahmed hurriedly ducked under the table and tried to get it away from him. It was a wonderful game. All the Fuzzies joined in on the other end and dragged Ahmed ten feet before he finally gave up and let go.

Meanwhile, Mike and Mitzi decided to scamper up the steps behind the bench where the judge was seated. When the judge looked up from the scene in front of him, Mitzi was showing the court all the things in her shoulder bag. The judge lifted Mitzi down from her spot and then banged his gavel for the court to come to order.

When everything had quieted down at last, the judge began to speak.

"It is the considered opinion of this court that the Fuzzies have enough in common with us to be called our brothers."

Pappy Jack hugged Little Fuzzy close. Little Fuzzy looked up.

"*Heinta?*" he asked.

Pappy Jack grinned. "You're in, kid." he whispered. "You've just joined the people."

Everyone cheered and applauded, and the Fuzzies jumped up on the tables and took a bow.

That night at last, Pappy Jack went home with his Fuzzies. But he wasn't just plain Pappy Jack anymore. He was the Commissioner of Native Affairs with his staff—Little Fuzzy, Mama, Ko-Ko, Max, Mike, Mitzi, Baby Fuzzy and Cinderella.

Little Fuzzy snuggled closer in Pappy Jack's lap. They were going home, home to the Wonderful Place. They had seen many wonderful places since the night they had been put in the bags—the Science Center, and the Space Naval Center where they had met so many people and had so much fun. But now they were going back to the old Wonderful Place in the woods, where it had all started.

And now the Big Ones would put things in their ears and be able to understand them. Already Pappy Jack had learned some of their words. Little Fuzzy strained his eyes out of the window of the aircar, searching for the outline of the compound in the darkness.

It was a good thing. The Gashta would all find Big Ones to live with. They would protect them, and feed them the wonderful tree-bark food, and keep them safe. And the Gashta would pay the Big Ones back, too. First they would give them love and play with them to make them happy. And later, when they had learned how, they would give them their help, too.